BRIMSTONE SLIPSTREAM

MATT WEBER

COBBLER & BARD PRESS

Face-First Into the Conflagration

Being an Essay on History, Family, and the Illegal Racing of Dragons through City Thoroughfares; by Dr. Shenireen Agama

It's a scene from later in my interviews, but I can't think of a better place for it than here:

"In the 'stream we have three talismans," says the new mother. Her wife is rocking the baby to sleep, off in a back room shushing like a typhoon; we are seated at the dining table, lit softly by a glowing carving of a feathered serpent on the ceiling. "These date back to the Sky-Eaters, before your people or mine set foot on these shores."

She grasps the goggles dangling from her neck, sky-blue glass in battered leather. The lenses match her hair. "Nimiennë, protector of sight."

With more effort than it should take, she lifts her shoulders and shrugs the brown leather jacket from the back of the chair behind her, then twirls it so I can see the back: It's tooled with a slim-snouted dolphin, rendered in the blocky, two-dimensional old Kayalim style, the amaranth pink of its body stark on the black leather. "Nimaïvola, protector of the heart. Since it protects your heart, it needs to be infused with your animating force. Zaya's is an orca: power and single-mindedness. Mine's a boto, adaptability and guile."

"I'll take your word that all makes sense," I say. "What's the third?"

She reaches inside the jacket and draws out a squat knife. I flinch before I can stop myself. It's a beautiful piece of work, the back of the blade serrated and the flat inlaid with the outline of a winged serpent, in the same displayed attitude as the one on the ceiling but in a much different style, all slender curves and wicked barbs. "Nimiando-alunor, the protector when all else is lost. These days we just call it a saddle-knife."

"What's it for?" There's something hypnotic about the inlaid serpent; it's a gleaming purple-black I've never seen in metal before, which helps hide the fact that it's not particularly attractive and slightly off-center.

"So we can cut out of our saddles if we need to. The Sky-Eaters rode bareback, of course—but if you've crashed in the middle of the jungle and your leg's caught under a ton or two of dead dragon-meat, well…"

"Say no more," I say, frantically writing. "Really useful. Thank you."

Zaya Shearwater emerges from the back hallway, her blazing magenta hair tousled, flushed with victory. "The baby's asleep," she says. "I win." She looks over at her wife. "Blood of mine, don't stab the journalist, the paper'll charge us for a replacement."

Kiriki Shearwater's eyes have already closed, her body relaxed back into the chair.

***

THE HOUSE WAS THE second thing I asked Zaya Shearwater to show me. It's a Kayalim-built flat above a mate shop in Lilac Precinct, co-domiciled with a Celadon Precinct flat by the broodspire. From that description, you could imagine the kind of place a High House scion would rent while she puts the final touches on her experimental song cycle, and those of us who've been to a few such houses would see some similarities: The walls and floor are clad in big, battered planks of rich dark wood, with low ceilings decorated with animal hieroglyphics on the surface and geometric scrollwork on the cornices. But this place hasn't been redone the way a High House scion would do it, with lamps all over, the kitchen walled off from the parlor, and most of the private rooms merged with each other or a common space. I note this, early in my interview with

Zaya and her ground crew, and her wife and co-pilot Kiriki tells me this:

"It's a traditional Kayalim family home. It's built to serve the daily work of the family, so the kitchen is open and the common space is centered on the dining table. It accommodates guests, but it doesn't center them."

"That is not," I say unwisely, "what I expected to hear from a woman who bought her place with gambling winnings from the dangerous and illegal sport of dragon-racing."

Kiriki, who is easily seven years younger than me and two heads shorter, smiles at me the way a kind professor might at a hard-working student of moderate brightness who's just realized she's been going at the problem all wrong; and Zaya, in the corner of my eye, smiles at *her* the way I imagine an almond sapling does at the first raindrop of spring.

The first thing I asked Zaya to show me was the dragon.

***

AT ZAYA AND KIRIKI'S request, I won't name the precinct the stable is in, or describe its surroundings. I can describe the interior, which has less the air of a farm or prison than you'd expect; the wyrms have individual enclosures, which themselves are only partly enclosed, so air can circulate and the dragons have sight-lines to one another. They're fed regularly and they have a few tough toys to keep them occupied—huge logs to chew and burn, balls to bat around, springs two fingers thick with boulders at either end. The proprietor, whom I'll call Fsalaan to protect their privacy, explains the five rules of the stable as I marvel at the peace and calm that reigns in this warehouse full of massive feathered lizards:

1. Pay your rent on time.

2. Common dragons only: Dawn Wyrms, Dusk Stalker Wyrms, Ranger Wyrms, and Eyrie Shrike Wyrms.

3. Any dragon who isn't fed on time is out.

4. Any dragon who doesn't leave to exercise once a week is

out.

5. Any dragon who attacks another dragon is out.

"Rule 5 is most important," says Fsalaan, as they walk me and Zaya to the enclosure of the dragon known in the 'stream as the Mule. ("The 'stream" is the brimstone slipstream, which which kicks you in the face like a mad ostrich as soon as your wyrm hits racing speed and doesn't abate until you land or else fall off your wyrm from the stench; how this term has become a metonymy for the entire dragon-racing scene is beyond me.) "Rules 2 through 4 are ways to get to 5. Common dragons are gregarious, they know each other. They don't test each other unless there's something to fight over or there's nothing else to do. As for the feed rule: Every 'streamer has their special diet that they swear makes their wyrm fart propitious breezes and shit bricks of diamond mortared with gold. I can't manage all that and I don't want to, but I won't let a wyrm starve in my stable. So if you're late, I'm going to stuff your wyrm full of the cheapest tilapia or cane-rat I can find at the night market, I'm going to bill you like it was the very Diadem of House Tuatara, you're going to take a very happy, logy dragon to your next race, and you're going to thank me for my services like you mean it."

I infer, out loud, that Rule 1 is the least important. I'm expecting some kind of stinging riposte, but Fsalaan just nods. "If I wanted clients who could pay on time, I'd set up in some middlebrow Mrineen precinct, admit exotic dragons, provide diet consultations... and then get stiffed twice as often as I do now, because I'd pull in a bunch of forever amateurs just burning cash. House Shearwater values what I do. They might not always come through on time, but they come through. And it's a pleasure to host fine wyrms like my good friend the Mule."

As if on cue, a head rises to peek above the enclosure labeled with the Mule's name.

What strikes me immediately is how normal it looks—facial skin and scales sun-faded from azure to sky blue, a rich magenta crest and slightly duller pink feathers on its neck, the size of its head and length of its neck entirely unremarkable for any Dawn Wyrm you might see circling over the bay, or couriering a few bushels of barley from an outlying farm. It puffs out a cloud of bright yellow smoke and fixes me with an orange eye. I ask Zaya and Kiriki whether it's all right to toss it a dried anchovy, then do so. A couple of other close-by dragons have taken an interest, a slightly slimmer Dawn Wyrm and a Dusk Stalker in faded indigo plumage.

Up close, the Mule remains obdurately average to the untutored onlooker, but Zaya happily speaks to its peculiarities. Carrying herself and Kiriki, she observes with a pointed look up at me, isn't as hard as you might think relative to carrying a single well-fed Mrineen, and the load is better distributed—but it is still a little hard, and seconds count at the front of these races, so they have to compensate for the added weight.

Some of that is in the build of the Mule, which is stocky and long-winged for a racing wyrm.

Some of it is in the minds of Zaya and Kiriki Shearwater, the first Kayalim empaths ever to compete at the highest levels of the 'stream: Their psionic link to the Mule comes with a reaction time that's an order of magnitude or two faster than conventional reins and pressure cues.

And some of it comes from the talents of their crew.

***

BACK AT HOUSE SHEARWATER (the name carved and painted into a beautiful sandalwood sign on their door, courtesy of Jinako te-Vala of Rust Precinct, who consented to be named in this report), Kiriki has gone to lie down and Zaya has left off her tea-making to burp the new baby, Jaliki, a serious and observant little person who seems deeply disturbed by whatever betrayal is currently playing out in their stomach and intestines. Perhaps it's their lamentations that bring a slim Ililuë woman out from one of the chambers, bleary-eyed but agreeable. With no words exchanged, Zaya hands her the baby, whose hysteria ebbs noticeably at the transfer, and she joins me, bouncing and patting, at the table.

Cerminir of Cildinior Amalgam is House Shearwater's physiologist, which means in practice that she's in charge of what the Mule puts in its gut. This isn't a thing that other 'streamers do—everyone basically knows brown rice for long races, white for short, and no rice in between, and anything beyond that is generally viewed as feckless nerdery. But feckless nerdery is Cerminir's baseline. She came to the Yemareir Agricultural College frustrated that a fertilizer of her innovation was only increasing cassava yields fourfold instead of sixfold, then worked through most of a doctorate before the bursar's office expelled her for nonpayment of tuition. She won't say much about her subsequent life on the dole except that there wasn't much of it: She soon joined the community of Ililuë street people in the Greens, where she found herself briefly posted to a work crew after getting caught raiding a trash bin outside an alchemist's shop for reagents she could use to track the advancement of her ketosis as she starved. She says she made her first contact with House Shearwater on that work crew, but she won't say who it was.

***

CS: YOU'RE THE REPORTER?

SA: That's right. I'm told you supervise every scrap of food that goes into the Mule.

CS: I can't vouch for any rats it might catch in the stable...

SA: Can you talk to our readers about how you use nutrition to make the Mule a better racer?

CS: What?

SA: How do you... I don't know, use food to make the Mule go faster?

CS: I don't know, how does Kiriki use her tits to make the nugget here grow bigger?

Cerminir holds the baby out in front of her, coos, and tosses them about three feet up; their head snaps alarmingly down at the throw, then up at the top of the arc, and three solid seconds pass before they regain the self-possession to begin bawling in Cerminir's face.

ZS: Cer, don't throw the nugget; his neck isn't strong enough. And be nice to the reporter. She knows you put the food inside the dragon. The question is what food and why.

CS: *I don't put the food inside the dragon, my arms aren't long enough.*

ZS: Cer.

Cerminir gazes very intensely at me.

CS: Dawn Wyrms are mostly fish-eaters, you could be forgiven for thinking they'd need hand-feeding for tougher fare. Or strange fare—can you imagine a face like that three feet into a vat of grape tomatoes, like? Or polenta?

ZS: *Cer.*

CS: Anyway, modern science, by which we mean the decontextualized and grievously contaminated scraps of truth that Mrineen colonial academic practice occasionally flakes off the epidermis of the world that is the case, would have you believe that—are you writing all this down?

SA, *frantically scrambling*: As much as I can.

CS: Why?

SA: I would very much like to publish an article about the Mule and its riders and crew, in no small part because I will be paid to do so.

Here, Cerminir gives me an apparently sincere look of interest that says, "Go on."

SA: In aid of that, I'd like to quote each member of the team talking about their area of expertise and how they contribute.

CS: I'm not telling you my meal plans.

SA: That's fine—it's about how you approach the work, not the details of what you do.

CS: I approach the work by feeding the Mule a set of very specific nutrients at precise times and doses in advance of the race, which I tune according to anything we know about the demands of the course and the strengths of the likely opposition—

SA: Exactly, that's perfect—

CS: —so I can't see how I can possibly help you, given that even a partial listing of the foods could easily, did you say that was perfect?

SA: Yes, and I'm a little distressed that you stopped just now.

CS: But that's obvious.

At this point Cerminir has entirely ceased to bounce Jaliki and is instead holding them the way you might hold a stray cat that that's just swallowed a diamond—the main thing is to make sure it doesn't bolt. Zaya brings a tray with a kettle and a mess of cups and straws in variable shapes and sizes; she picks up Jaliki and begins bouncing and cooing to them while Cerminir pours mate for both of us. I get a square-sided mug with a pretty vine pattern in muted green and gold; Cerminir takes a glossy black cup with a white interior and a large chip in the rim, which she deliberately rests her straw in as she drinks.

CS: All right, I've been thinking about your line of questioning and I think I understand why to some people it might not be obvious.

SA: I can't tell you how relieved I am to hear that.

CS: What I was saying earlier is that modern science, by which—

SA: —flakes off the epidermis of the world—

CS: Modern science holds that food does two things: You can build a wyrm with it, or you can move a wyrm with it. And we don't neglect those things; we need to make sure the Mule is strong, and we need its brain to be well supplied with—

ZS: Careful, Cer, that's telling—

CS: —*right*, with certain specific fatty acids whereof I may say no more, for maximum psionic receptivity. But there's a third thing you can do, with dragons, and that's push them to change. Everyone sort of knows about draconic somatoplasticity—

SA: —not me—

CS: OK, everyone knows that dragons' bodies adapt in response to stress. Fly through the White Springs and it'll grow a new coat of down, all that. For it to work, you need to pair a physical stress, like cold, with a mental stress, like feeling cold. And there are proteins and micronutrients that amplify the process. Of course, everyone also knows that this doesn't really work for speed, because you don't have the mental piece. They don't care if they win, they're just happy to fly.

SA: … so if you can't make dragons faster by leveraging their… so-ma-to-plasticity… why bother feeding them in a way that encourages them to change?

Cerminir graces me with a saturnine smile, then gets up, stretches, and walks over to Zaya. She gives Jaliki a kiss on the forehead, then hands them to her.

CS: That would be telling. Good night…

***

THE BRIMSTONE SLIPSTREAM, OR the 'stream to practitioners, is as old as Yemareir itself—or much older, depending on where you place the birth of… either one, I suppose? When Yymroun Tuatara first anchored the *Seeker* by the sands of Hascópa Bay and forged inland to discover the ruins we now call proto-Yemareir and the Ililuë amalgams who lived east and south of them, he became enthralled with the Sky-Eaters—a caste of holy fools, almost, whom the amalgams supported in their dragon-taming endeavors in exchange for stories, a look at their scars, and the hope of a tame dragon to help feed and defend their communities. Indeed, Captain Tuatara's journals from that maiden expedition barely mention anything else, which is why we look to the first mate's log and the windhauler's letters to his wife for details about that first contact between Mrineen and Ililuë.

But it was, famously, that enthrallment with the Sky-Eaters that led Yymroun Tuatara back to Mlinivoun to muster a colonial force, hoping to reconstitute the old empire's glory with new feathered dragons to replace the old wildfire dreadnoughts, two thousand years extinct even then. And that same enthrallment ran rampant among the defectors who chose to join House Tuatara on stolen ships to build a new city over the old. Racing through the ruins of the season-city that would become Yemareir, and the beautiful and abundant natural hazards around which it was built, was an occasional enthusiasm of the Ililuë Sky-Eaters; it was wyrm-fevered Mrineen colonists who codified the courses, rules, and etiquette of the races—though all, of course, have changed, as season-city grew into city-state and the towers of Yemareir grew alongside, and ultimately overshadowed, the broodspires.

The 'stream has been banned in one way or another for the balance of our history, but our city's founding is as bound up in it as the son's fetish in the father's dirty magazines. (NB: I am not a psychologist.) Wyrm-fever is why we have one broodspire per precinct, because Yymroun Tuatara imagined precinct alderwights principally as ministers to the broodspires and only secondarily as administrators; it's why those alderwights are formed into the House of the Stars, because Yymroun Tuatara wanted the voice of the dragons to balance the voice of the noble houses; it's why our seat of government is in Argent Precinct, because the Argent Swordwing was the wyrm most admired by Yymroun Tuatara.

And it's why Yymroun Tuatara first broke the Ililuë taboo of entering the area that would become Ashen Precinct during hatching season—prefiguring the challenge that would become the 'stream's ultimate race, the Grand Bisai, which House Shearwater is favored to win at 2-1 odds and rising.

***

I MEET YYRREEN SHEARWATER in another precinct I will not name here. It's an outlying precinct, though, full of apartments and businesses that must have been busy and vital a century or two ago, when we couldn't build as high and hadn't lost half a generation to war. There's no shortage of squatters here, but no police presence, and no one who sees us will go out of their way to snitch; they have too little to gain from talking to police, and too much to lose. Yyrreen is short and wiry, sharp-featured but wide-eyed, with black hair in a loose ponytail; she dresses in bright, loose lines, heavy on turquoise and rust-red, with silver bangles and a chunky silver necklace—in short, like a traditional Kayalim, which her affiliations declare she is not. It's only the costume, though, that betrays her Kayalim ancestry. Put her in a purple sheath skirt and a tight silver halter and I, at least, would take her for Mrineen without a second thought.

SA: How do the dragons get out here?

YS: Come on now, Agama-*cha*, buy me dinner first.

SA: Fine. Please describe your role in the House Shearwater ground crew.

YS: I put together training courses for the Mule to fly.

SA: And what's special about that?

YS: We can end this interview right now if you want.

SA: Come on now, Shearwater-*cha*, you know what I'm asking. Why can't Zaya and Kiriki just go out to the desert and stretch the Mule's wings? They must have studied the courses as closely as you have—

YS: Sure, they study. But—look, take the Mariposa Annulus, a couple months back. That goes through Cadmium, Incarnadine, Alabaster—not to mention the Fountain itself, which is basically always full of people wanting to have a nice peaceful walk and enjoy the scenery. You can't just practice that route.

SA: Why not?

YS: Because you can't.

SA: Imagine, for a moment, that I don't have the background knowledge to understand why that makes a speck of sense. I don't think I've ever seen a police wyrm within shouting distance of the Rosewing Fountain

YS: If we run the route once, it's fine. But what kind of practice is that? So maybe we run it a few times. Still not a huge problem, but that's a lot more citizens in these respectable bourgeois precincts getting buzzed by death chickens. But are we the only 'streamers with the bright idea to practice a course beforehand? An individual without *background knowledge* might not realize that it could occur to, I don't know, every idiot who's even thought about saddling up a dragon and getting—

SA: All right, I see your point. So what are we doing out here? Have you got some kind of practice course?

YS: We've got records of the Mule's weak spots in dozens of races. You know how Zaya and Kiriki have a reputation for showing up late to the after-parties?

SA: … clearly I've been interviewing the wrong people.

YS: It's because they're sitting with me while I scrape every fleck of memory from their brains before the beer and arrack wash it all away. Anyway, we cross-reference those weak points with the maps of whatever race is coming next, and then I come out here or to a precinct like it and we hash out a course to hit those weak points as hard as I can.

SA: And how did that job fall to you?

YS: I walked up to Kiriki and told me she needed me to do it if she wanted to win.

SA: Say more.

YS: The boy I was sleeping with took me to Heliotrope Precinct to watch his friend race. We're crammed on the balcony of some other friend's dole-flat, ten floors up, and I see a Dawn Wyrm with two Kayalim girls on it round a corner as gracefully as a dream. They pass the balcony, almost close enough to touch. I can see the scratches on their goggles; I can smell the sulfur on the dragon's breath.

… and then some Eyrie Shrike with an obviously drunk Mrineen boy on it snaps around the corner and overtakes them, and all these idiots crowded onto the balcony cheer like jackals at a carcass; and the boy I was sleeping with turns to me and says—*I quote*—"Did you see my boy Virsoon just sneak-fuck those bricklayer sluts?"

So I tossed him over the balcony, left the party, found Zaya and Kiriki, and told them I wouldn't be able to live with myself unless I found a way to help them corner better, and also I didn't have a place to sleep because my boyfriend was lying in an alley in Heliotrope Precinct with all his bones broken. They let me share their dole-flat, and I've lived with them ever since. Which is fabulous, because otherwise, I'd probably be living right about there.

Yyrreen gestures to indicate a tall tenement.

YS: I found a key outside it once and spent all day testing doors. One of them works—at least one, I stopped at one. Until someone breaks the door down in the hope of loot, that's my bolt-hole.

SA: Can I see the key?

Yyrreen draws a thong out of the neckline of her dress, one I hadn't noticed behind the necklace. It is a rust-pitted, badly scratched iron key, three times the size of anything you'd see in use today and far less complex, a single flap with an intricate cutout rather than a finely machined row of teeth.

YS: Someone'll break the door down eventually. But not today.
SA: Why not?
YS: Wyrm'll scare the squatters off.

Yyrreen is looking behind me; at once I notice a soft, rhythmic sound growing in my ears like the rush of an oncoming breaker, and a faint rotten-egg smell also, though more slowly, intensifying. I turn to see the Mule tearing down ___ Street in its racing posture—feathers of its crest and neck lying flat, wing-arms blooming into cyan-and-violet fans, then disappearing as they haul the Mule through the air, leaving cyclones of street debris skirling in its wake. The front rider—Zaya, I think—lies on her stomach, pine-green hair whipping in the jetstream over her goggled face. The Mule roars past me, a wing snapping back not an inch before it would have hit my face; the wind of its wake nearly knocks me down. It smells like sulfur and rotted fish. As if it's made its point, it wheels around and spreads its wings to brake, then floats down almost daintily. Zaya dismounts expertly, clearing the eight or nine feet from the Mule's shoulders to the street with no more evident effort than I would use to step down a flight of stairs. The orca on her jacket ripples gracefully when her feet hit the ground.

YS: Where's your lover?
ZS: Nursing Jaliki. He was a terror last night.
YS: I didn't hear him.
ZS: That's why we thank the Sculptor for walls.

Yyrreen and Zaya both glance, swiftly but unmistakably, at me.

ZS: We'll just stretch the Mule's wings a bit. It's earned an easy practice for once.

YS: Whatever you like.

***

LOOKING AT THE MAP, you could be forgiven for thinking the Grand Bisai is not much different from, say, the Harrow Spiral—and, indeed, the course is similar, even arguably less challenging, as it skips the Caldera and the Bone Loom and plots no set path through Ashen Precinct; 'streamers need only enter it at one marked gate and leave it at the other. But the real difference—the one that defines the Bisai—is in the timing.

Anyone who's dwelt in this city more than a year or two has seen, or participated in, one of the great migrations driven by the draconic brooding cycle. Although no human of my acquaintance was present at the hatching of the Mule, we know it is twenty-five years old, because Dawn Wyrms breed on eleven-year cycles of which the last was three years ago. (Cognoscenti will use the term "third-cohort" for such a wyrm; a first-cohort Dawn Wyrm is three years old at this writing, a second-cohort Dawn Wyrm fourteen, and so on; in eight years, a new cohort will hatch and the Mule, at thirty-three, will be fourth-cohort.) The Mule's precinct of provenance is unknown, but Dawn Wyrms almost always brood in the spires at Cobalt, Ultramarine, Heliotrope, and Lilac Precincts. So the Mule's parents met each other for a brief golden moment about twenty-six and a half years ago, perhaps in Lilac Precinct, whose residents would obligingly have moved to linked domiciles and dole-flats in other precincts out of phase with the Dawn Wyrm breeding cycle, typically Incarnadine, Madder, Celadon, and Alabaster. The broodspires in Incarnadine, for example, are typically used by Eyrie Shrike Wyrms, who breed on a thirteen-year cycle, which is why co-domicile contracts for Lilac and Incarnadine have a provision for housing rights in a dole-flat in Damask every 143 years, when the Dawn and Eyrie breeding cycles coincide...

... but this is a level of complexity well out of scope for this article on illegal street dragon racing. It suffices to say that we do all of this because living next door to a bunch of dragons in estrus is a prayer for death. Contrariwise, living near newly hatched dragons is not all that dangerous, but it is unbelievably annoying. Young dragons are too dumb and hungry not to attack children and pets, fall to their deaths off roofs, fly into windows, get stuck in sewer gratings, set trash-heaps on fire, or kill each other and leave half-eaten dragon carcasses in the streets, which attracts rats, jackals, buzzards, feral dogs, and more dragons. Since both breeding and hatching seasons are unlivable for humans, we typically don't move back in between them, which leaves (for the Mule) probably a three-year period in which the usual residents of Lilac Precinct pulled up stakes, to return when the Dawn Wyrms of what is now the third cohort had thinned out, spread out, and grown up.

All of which brings us to the matter of Ashen Precinct.

The Cinereal Vore Wyrms of Ashen Precinct languish for nearly three years in their shells before they hatch, but their seven-year brood-cycle is shorter than those of the common wyrms, longer only than the Pileated Dwarf Wyrms of Russet Precinct, which is why no one both resides and owns property in Russet Precinct. The Vores emerge from these eggs, which are as long as a tall Mrineen man, able to use their fire-breath within minutes and to fly within an hour; and they are ravenous. Perhaps one in five, or one in ten, will survive the hatching season. They leave Ashen when they are strong enough to climb higher in the sky than the ancient sorcerous runes on the precinct's border-wall can reach. The remainder will be eaten by their cohort, who are thorough devourers with stomach acids potent enough to digest bone and scales. The Grand Bisai is timed for the middle of that hatching season, by which time the new Vore cohort will have diffused through the precinct like a drop of blood in a glass of water.

Those of you who share our ancestral obsession with flying killer lizards will need no further explanation when I mention the Trials of Vnaleen Tuatara. For the rest of you: Vnaleen Tuatara was a bored heiress with tendencies running bloody-minded and mathematical, and she somehow—she lived less than a century after her ancestors broke ground on the House Ignohalic in what would become Argent Precinct—got hold of a clutch of hatchling Cinereal Vores. She pitted each, one by one, against successively older dragons in a given breed until the Vore was killed.

Against Dusk Stalker and Ranger wyrms, the hatchling Vore killed the third-cohort wyrm, but sustained injuries grave enough that the fourth-cohort wyrm defeated it without much trouble.

Against Dawn Wyrms, the hatchling defeated the fourth-cohort wyrm. Vnaleen Tuatara could not find someone who would sell her a fifth.

✳✳✳

Kirono Shearwater has to be rousted from his room for the interview. Zaya and Jaliki do the honors; I hear squealing and cooing after they enter, and low loving words in a man's voice. But when he emerges—short, slight, and smooth-faced for a Kayalim, with chin-length hair dyed a deep rose, dressed in a stained violet waistcoat and loose trousers, a style imported or at least aped from the Pearl Isles—he looks tired and anxious, periodically sucking on his bitten-nailed fingertips as though he has been recently burned.

Kirono is House Shearwater's aerodynamicist, a lapsed doctoral student in materials science at the Initheen Taipan College of Engineering and Natural Philosophy. He grew up in Viridian Precinct, only child of a pair of up-and-coming restaurateurs riding the north-facing wave of gentrification; but he left home early in his teens, and spent some time on the dole in Rust and Damask Precincts before beginning his studies. I assume out loud at some point that he and Cerminir would have known each other while they were in school, but he denies it. Different disciplines, different institutions. When I ask, at that later interview, whether they might have met on a work crew stationed at a penal farm, he looks at me like I've just blown my nose on his lapel. But we're getting ahead of ourselves.

SA: Tell me about feathers.

KS: Well, ah, dragons. They—let me back up; birds. Have you ever spent a minute watching someone's pet bird? It's hard to observe birds in the city; they're always running away from drag-ons—

SA: As a surrogate for my least informed reader, let's pretend I haven't.

KS: Least informed…? Ahh, right. *[Kirono takes a long pull from his cup of mate with a noticeably unsteady hand, then winces at the heat on his mouth.]*

SA: I'm a reporter; I'm writing a piece—

KS: No, I know, it just… helps if I can forget that.

SA: I'll try not to draw attention to… myself?

KS: I appreciate that. *[He takes a more moderate sip, although his hand still shakes a bit.]* If you watch a pet bird—any bird—or any dragon—for long enough, you'll see them preen. The Mule, like, has glands in the base of its neck that secrete a sort of oil and a sort of wax, and that smooths out feathers and aligns them and helps them do what they need to do, which is stay light, grip the air when they need to, and slide through it when they need to.

Now, on the one hand, that oil and wax has been calibrated by… conservatively, hundreds of thousands of years of adaptation? To the dragon's needs. So it's hard to do better and easy to do worse. But the dragon's needs—those it's adapted to through the millennia—don't really include racing. *How* un-adapted depends on the dragon; Dawns and Rangers are natural gliders, so their wax is thinner and weaker; Dusks and Shrikes are sprinters who do hunt agile prey, so they have a thick wax that keeps their feathers in place through strong wind shears and quick changes of direction… *[KS stares, frowning, into space for a moment; he seems to have lost the thread.]*

SA: So where do you come in?

KS: Oh, I make better wax.

SA: How?

ZS: No trade secrets, please.

KS, *shuddering momentarily*: Let me think about this for a second.

Zaya doesn't quite reach across the table to take his hand, but she puts her hand out flat, palm down, almost as if she had.

ZS: Hey, it's OK. You're doing fine.

Kirono gives Zaya a look that's obviously trying to say "I got this" but comes out much more "Lady, have you met me?" I feel momentarily bad for putting this obviously anxious person on the spot, but then I think about the opportunity to write sentences like the one before this one and my heart lightens. Don't trust journalists, kids, we're not good people.

But the tension is broken by Kiriki emerging from her room. She doesn't look rested; she hugs herself and shivers for a moment, although it is of course midsummer and even the breezes coming in through the windows feel hot as wyrm-flame. She takes a chair next to Zaya and rests her head on her shoulder, but doesn't close her eyes.

ZS: Everything OK?

Kiriki: Fine. Just couldn't sleep.

KS: So you can't go wrong with stronger and lighter for the most part—in theory you can, but generally a wax that's stronger for the same weight is better. If the race has a lot of tight cornering, maybe you accept a little more weight for more strength. It's the environmental factors that make it really interesting. I have a heat-resistant compound, an extra-strong one for high winds—or, for example, the really popular wax for Dawns is half the weight and ten times the strength of their natural compound, but it's prone to washing off in water, especially salt water. So you don't want to use it on, say, the Blue Path because you've got to get through the Sea-Queen's Gate before you do the Bone Loom, and if you use that wax your Dawn is going to look like a chicken that's been shaken to death by a fox, which is what it will fly like as well. There's another wax that's almost as good and waterproof, but most Dawns won't go near it.

Kirono is visibly proud here. I make a guess.

SA: But the Mule will?

ZS, *lightly*: Don't answer that, please.

Kirono looks at me and shrugs, it seems like in relief. I steal a glance at Zaya, who smiles knowingly.

Kiriki: We're able to do what we do because we work together. The Mule's as much a part of that as the rest of us.

ZS: I was trying to help here.

Kiriki: I know. But it's all right. We're here today because they won't do what we do, not because they can't. And we don't have to do it for much longer.

ZS: Heart of mine—

Jaliki has begun to whine and reach for Kiriki. She holds her hands out for them; when Zaya hands them over, she frees a breast and lets them suck. The baby's latch seems to release something inside Kiriki: Her shoulders drop, her thighs relax, the muscles of her face slacken, draping her skin like thin linen against her skull. She does not open her eyes to speak; her voice is perceptibly weary.

Kiriki: Breath of mine, it's fine.

An uncomfortable silence reigns.

SA: If I can ask Kirono one more question—will you be using the heat-resistant wax in the Bisai? In case, the scales of Heaven shield you, the Mule should take a hit from a Vore?

KS: Well—

Kiriki: No. There's no wax under the stars that's going to protect your wyrm from a direct hit from a Vore. Take a hit like that and your first option is: Get out of Ashen any way you can. If you can't do that, you fight. Or just sit and wait to die, it probably amounts to the same thing.

SA: Are you worried about that happening to you?

I see Kiriki's head drooping down her chest even as I ask the question. It reaches that point where your body realizes it's about to keel over and wakes you up; her head snaps back up and she look me in the eyes. After a moment, she smiles.

Kiriki: Of course. You don't survive Ashen Precinct in hatching season without worrying a little. But not as much I worry about making rent, or making sure this person gets enough to eat.

Kiriki's arms are bare, so I can see her biceps contract, her knuckles whitening just the slightest bit, as she pulls the baby to her.

***

ANOTHER CONTRIBUTION OF THE scholar-heiress Vnaleen Tuatara was her discovery of the benefits of cooking. She did this by a means that will be familiar: She took a small brood of snakes, split it into two and fed one on raw meat and the other on the same (raw) weight of cooked meat. The snakes fed on cooked meat grew larger. This, she claimed, solved the mystery of dragonfire; it is no more than a means of extracting the maximum nutrition from prey.

(This rationale, it's worth noting, is a subject of disgust to the physicists I interviewed to confirm it. The obvious objection is that searing-hot flame takes more energy to produce than it could possibly buy back in metabolic efficiency. To a reporter unschooled in computation, their calculations seemed convincing enough. When I asked why I hadn't found any reports to this effect in the proceedings of the various learned societies of dracobiophysics—which are, gentle reader, *surprisingly numerous*—the uniform answer was that no editor and no publisher of such a journal would dare cast the shade of doubt on a famous result from a scion of House Tuatara. In any case, no editor or publisher of such a journal would comment on the matter to me on or off the record, so there it stands.)

... be all that as it may, the Cinereal Vore Wyrm does not roast its prey for that reason, or really at all. Rather, it carbonizes it, with a fire hot enough to melt metal and stone. How the creature derives nutrition from the flaking embers of meat is a mystery on which even Vnaleen Tuatara declined to speculate.

The first record of the Vore's practice of comprehensive charring was provided by Xyvveen Amphisbaena, the wife of Captain

Yymroun of the *Seeker*, who unwisely led the search for the said Captain's remains in the part of the season-city that would become Ashen Precinct. Her survival was a matter of dumb luck. Yymroun had ridden in on Dvitvar, a Ranger Wyrm that, if modern sizing can be relied on, must have been in the eighth cohort, based on its reputation for bringing down grown rhinoceros and plucking saltwater crocodiles from the delta. A swarm of Vore hatchlings can bring down an adversary that size, targeting vulnerable regions like the wings and face; but their losses will be heavy, and the survivors will not eat it quickly. The captain's wife got close enough to identify Dvitvar's half-eaten corpse before she turned her own wyrm around. Yymroun was burned black from head to foot.

The discovery of the Vore Wyrms in Ashen Precinct nearly halted the construction of the city. Certainly it sent many of the pilgrims on boats back to Mlinivoun or on caravans east and south into the continent. The immediate question, of course, was why none of these terrifying wyrms had been seen outside the precinct grounds. The pilgrim sorcerers quickly discovered the wards on the low walls that surround the precinct, but how they work is still unknown. No sorcerer of Yemareir, at least, has been able to produce a ward selective to any dragon species, Vore or otherwise. But, through more than a hundred breeding cycles, the wards have held—even as no other species of wyrm has had any trouble crossing them in the Grand Bisai, or any other time.

***

HAVING LEARNED THIS MUCH about the city of stone huts and broodspires that preceded Yemareir, it's been impossible for me not to wonder more about what it was like. There are few answers on offer, though, and they serve less to illuminate than to show the extent of what still languishes in shadow.

Everyone knows proto-Yemareir as a "season-city," although our schooling is not always clear on what that means. It was not a permanent settlement, but a periodic one. It seems likely that the human migration to Yemareir was driven initially by the salmon migration through the Ilweran River, and likely ended when the proto-Yemari departed to catch the northern endpoint of the wildebeest migration, a hundred miles to the south, or else the pawpaw harvest on the eastern side of the continent.

It is clear that different cultures met, and built, in the season-city; burials with no less than five distinct sets of cultural markers attested elsewhere on the continent have been unearthed, and somewhere between eleven and fourteen different forms of writing and pictographs have been discovered. There seem to be, broadly, about three different schools of broodspire architecture, and other structures show countless variations. Although it is common to hear the season-city described as a city of spires and huts, innumerable types of structures preexisted contemporary Yemareir—single- and multi-family residences, shrines, mess-halls, dormitories, longhouses, sweat-lodges, stables, hutong, libraries—and the skeleton of our city's roadways still originates from the footpaths present in proto-Yemareir.

Very little of the writing, and none of the bones, bears any resemblance to what one might find among the nearby Ililuë amalgams, all of whose lore refers to pre-Mrineen Yemareir as nothing more than a ruin.

But where does this all leave us? If the Ililuë know anything about the roamers who built the season-city, they aren't telling; thanks to Mrineen colonization, there aren't many of them to talk in any case. The season-city's builders left all the signs of human civilization, and also several dozen stone towers (in at least three distinct architectural styles) for dragons to abandon eggs in—and then, in Ashen Precinct, a single deployment of sorcerous technology that no Mrineen, Kayalim, or Ililuë has been able to approximate, much less duplicate, in most of a thousand years.

Think about that for a moment. To contain the Vore Wyrm menace, the builders chose to deploy a measure so far beyond the present state of the art in sorcery that the theory doesn't exist to account for it, when they could simply have destroyed the broodspire. They bent over backwards so that Cinereal Vore Wyrms could keep their place in the heart of the city.

No wonder we put down roots here. Even over the gulf of millennia, we know wyrm-fever when we see it; and we thrill to it.

✳✳✳

MS: THE CLOSEST I'VE ever gotten to a dragon is the audience area by the starting gate. I don't share the ancestral fetish. But do I like money.

Minshoon Shearwater is the tallest resident of this house by rather more than a head, and his shoulders are broad for his size; his chest is large, his arms muscled like a stonemason's. He should seem out of place in this house, sized and decorated for the Kayalim who now sit together in it with their sleeping child, but he does not: He gracefully navigates the slightly-too-small furniture, and his height is not cramped but merely snug in the low ceilings. He entered the dining room, when Zaya summoned him, with a sheaf of papers that I thought, at first, were receipts. As he sorted them into piles on the table, I saw that they were odds—odds and names. Jaliki has fallen asleep at the breast. It looks like Kiriki's joined them, but every so often I catch her looking through slitted eyelids.

SA: Forgive a naïf, but—the Mule is widely acknowledged as the favorite to win the Bisai. Can you make money betting on it any more?

MS: I don't have to. There's no shortage of odds for second place.

SA: You're not seriously going to tell me you won't take odds on the women you call your family.

MS: They are my family, and it depends on the odds.

SA: This is going to be published, you know. You're speaking for the historical record here.

MS: I have odds on the first-second spread. I've made good money on that before.

ZS: Betting against us?

MS: What can I say? Pair of charismatic young ladies come up in the 'stream, a certain type of gambler's apt to get overconfident about the margin. Dumb money spends just as well as smart, but you have to win it first.

SA: Your fans will be crushed.

MS: I mean, odds do flatten out a bit for the Bisai—
SA: Why's that?
MS: —because 'streamers getting killed has a sort of overall randomizing effect on the results. Have to price that into your model.

Here, shorthand fails me on "randomizing" and it's several seconds before I look up to register Minshoon's expression, which is caught in limbo between amusement and fury—a strangely Mrineen expression on a man so firmly immured in a home and family so profoundly, if not classically, Kayalim.

SA: Haha, I can see how that might—
MS: It's interesting that you find that funny. We're talking about the deaths of people in this room. Mothers, actually. There's a market pricing the probability of a Cinereal Vore Wyrm just casually orphaning that tiny child in Kiriki's arms. His name is Jaliki.
SA: I know.
MS: He's not off the breast yet. He needs to nurse to live.
SA: I know.
MS: Do you know how far into her pregnancy Kiriki was still racing?
SA: No.
MS: What about after? How soon after his birth did Kiriki get back on the Mule to race, do you know?
SA: No.
MS: You're a reporter, *why the fuck not?*
ZS: Minshoon, you're right and I love you for it, but you're performing for yourself here and I'm asking you to stop.

Minshoon flares his nostrils, puffs his chest out as if he's about to shout a hole through the ceiling, then lets it all out—or seems to—with a swift shutting of his eyes. When they open, they are not calm; his face is no less angry than it was a moment ago; but he is in control.

MS: Zaya's right. This isn't helping anyone. What's your name?

I give it.

MS: Is it all right if I ask two more questions? I understand the shoe's usually on the other foot.

I nod.

MS: What magazine will this appear in?
SA: *The Damask Free Press.*
MS: Why did your editor want it?
SA: *City Crypt* and *Transpiring* saw huge jumps in sales when they reported on the 'stream. Kayalim women and young Mrineen men were especially interested.
MS: You've probably saturated the market for Kayalim women already.
SA: Don't sell your family short. They're very inspiring.
MS: Well said.

He grins and raises his cup of mate in appreciation.

MS: But, look, your growth opportunity's in Heliotrope and Celadon and Ultramarine, not out in the Pinks. This is entertainment for Mrineen man-boys with cash to spare on learning soirée trivia about the weird and illegal habits of the other half. Mass market ethology, slumming without the slum—
SA: That's not what it is.
MS: Will you print this conversation?
SA: I'll include it when I file. Whether it gets printed isn't up to me.
MS: That's at least half honest. Why would you include it?
SA: If I say "because you want me to," I fail your test, right?

Minshoon smiles again and raises his cup.

SA: How's this, then: I think the market of Kayalim women you say we've saturated might appreciate what you have to say.
ZS: Don't be so sure.
MS: Her, you should listen to.

SA: Final question. Ever been sentenced to a work crew?
MS: Do you ask everyone that question?
SA: You're not the first. It's OK if you'd rather not answer.
MS: Suspended sentence. Never actually did a tour.
SA: Thanks.
MS: You don't want to ask me what for?
SA: You want to tell me?
MS: No, but I like to be asked.

I drop my eyes to write down our last exchange, and something in the air between us that says we're done. I move the pen longer than I strictly have to, spying a little. His eyes have drifted to the odds scattered on the table. They alight on a sequence of scraps; he mouths what I have to assume is a number. Across the table, Jaliki pulls off the breast, squirms, then squalls; Minshoon gets up and swiftly lifts them from Kiriki's arms, putting them up on his shoulder and clapping them on the back as he walks across the common room to put some distance between fussing child and sleeping mother. She isn't sleeping, though. Her eyes move under slitted eyelids. Zaya sees it, too, and she sees me seeing it.

***

THERE ARE SO MANY eddies of history I could fetch up in at this point—anyone following the 'stream over the last two seasons will appreciate how detail accumulates, and how hard it is to understand why anything has happened unless you're steeped in all the things nobody bothers to write down for observers six months later, still less years and centuries. But Minshoon's barbs have dug in, as I can only guess they were meant to, and as I draw nearer to the main event of this increasingly frothy slurry of inconclusive dialogue and half-relevant background I'm finding it more and more difficult to view what I have learned through any other lens than his.

Let me, then, observe a thing that everyone knows and no one—or no Mrineen—cares to talk about. Most 'streamers and most champions are Mrineen, but the builders of the streets through which the 'stream runs are Kayalim—and the first Kayalim to win the Grand Bisai will do so, if they do, thanks to a lore developed in and passed down from their indenture.

"Indenture" is a vexed term this century, although it was not always—there was a time, before anyone reading this was born, when citizens of Yemareir owned up to what our state had done to the Kayalim who originally came here to build around the broodspires, to replace season-huts with dole-flats and pave and tend the boulevards that once were linear orchards. Now it is fashionable to question that once-fixed wisdom—to take seriously the Doctrine of Return, which justified denial of the franchise to Kayalim even when Mrineen had fought beside Kayalim to secure it; to invoke the fact that they were willing migrants as though it justifies abuse at their destination.

It is well known that the Kayalim pilgrims crossed the ocean to Yemareir fleeing ostracism and death for unholy sorcery, the pogroms of a paranoid king. It is less well known who supplied them with the ships. Zitan te-Akoyo, a trader and shipbuilder in Kayazē, had studied in Mlinivoun alongside Tvareen Ferdelance, the Minister of Operations for the Yemareir that was not yet built. In their correspondence, te-Akoyo spoke of the pogroms of the Kayalim empaths, and Ferdelance identified a use for them.

In Kayazē, there are no megafauna. Empaths there used their talents principally to bind monkeys as servants and familiars, and to train the region's resplendent feathered serpents in the ritual dances of their faith. Yemareir, in contrast, is infested with irritable beasts of terrifying size and strength: great apes, ground sloths, rhinoceros, and so on. It takes no special genius to realize that a foreman who can order a rhinoceros around is going to outbuild any competitor stuck working exclusively with hairless apes, which complain ceaselessly and sometimes engage in collective bargaining. So Tvareen Ferdelance began funneling great tides of cash over to Kayazē, and Zitan te-Akoyo got into the asylum business, with empaths allowed to jump the line for the ships to Yemareir.

But Ferdelance and te-Akoyo understood neither the animals they sought to control nor the people they brought in to do it. No force of nature and no Kayalim psionics can make a bull hippopotamus anything other than a fountain of incontinence and homicide, and our archives have the death certificates to prove it. Even the more biddable giants of the veldt, like ground sloths and gorillas, would ultimately go berserk from agoraphobia and an excess of industry; animals that size are accustomed to long periods of idleness in small cadres of friends and relatives, not ceaseless drudgery alongside a sea of chattering apes. Alone of the indigenous megafauna, elephants responded well enough to Kayalim psionics—they are patient and untiring workers, and for whatever reason they seem to tolerate concentrations of architecture and humanity that scorch the brain-pans of other animals.

The toll on the empaths themselves, though, would take a few years to manifest. Their means of communicating with the capuchins and winged boomslangs of Kayazē were fixed by ritual and honed by long history. The minds of Yemareir's great apes and ungulates were not so different that connection was impossible... but they were different enough that the old methods provided little protection to the minds of the empaths.

The foremen of Yemareir dismissed the consequent dementias among the empaths as "tusk-madness," and joked with some pride that the elephants of Yemareir were stronger of mind than the beasts of Kayazē. Over the two centuries of hard building that fleshed out the bones of the season-city into roughly what we know as Yemareir, those dementias diminished—unnoticed by the foremen or any other Mrineen at the time. We know of it only from the Kayalim Books of Departure, archived and collated by Kaano te-Jizan of Madder Precinct, and a few terribly late studies of the evolution of Kayalim empathic ritual in the proto-Yemareir period.

The ritual optimizations that account for the decline in empathy-induced dementia are thinly documented; there is an old and potent current of fear that, if Mrineen learn empathy for animals, they will decide at long last that they have no need for Kayalim. But the most effective optimization is so simple that it needs no writing down. To avoid tusk-madness, instead of one ritual practitioner, have two.

✳✳✳

THE KEEN-EYED READER WILL have gathered, by now, that the same thing works for dragons.

***

ZS: WHEN MY FATHERS were broke, they'd go out to the bay and get a wild Dawn to help them knock over liquor stores. A Dawn won't get drunk on a fifth of whiskey, but they like it as much as halibut, and it's less suspicious to get caught with.

Having burped Jaliki into a sort of squirmy contentment, Minshoon has deposited him with Zaya and retreated with his papers to his quarters. I'd have believed Kiriki was asleep, too, except that she smiled at Zaya's description of her fathers. She seems to realize I'm on to her, and opens her eyes, half-lidded.

The contrast between them isn't something anyone could fail to notice, but it's impossible not to say a few words about. They are similar heights, but Zaya is broad-shouldered, narrow-waisted, and strong-thighed; Kiriki, even after giving birth, is slight and wide-eyed, her expressive features somehow more enigmatic than Zaya's still, flat ones. They are both long-haired, in defiance of the customary Kayalim cropped styles; they dress in a conscious mingling of traditional Kayalim colors and typical Mrineen cuts, although they do not wear jewelry. Zaya's hair is dyed the same pink as the feathers on the Mule's head and neck; Kiriki's is the sky blue of its back, although her black roots are showing. I have just asked Zaya how she came to join the 'stream.

ZS: I wish I could tell you that was some funny story they told me when I was old enough to hear it, but I'm not old enough to hear it now. I can't remember a time when the two of them were out and I didn't think they might be thieving with a dragon again.

Kiriki: You do not.

ZS: Don't what?

Kiriki: Wish you could tell the nice lady that you hadn't seen your dads' bullshit first-hand. You love scandalizing polite society with this stuff.

Zaya gives a "guilty as charged" shrug here.

ZS: Love it or loathe it, it's the one thing I learned from them. Neither of them was much of an empath on their own. They definitely couldn't go mind-to-mind with a wyrm solo.

SA: How did you get from apprentice booze-thief to the fastest woman in the city?

ZS, *laughing*: Like that's a big promotion. Look, I spent a lot of my childhood in the Tvashaan Basilisk project—that's the one in Madder Precinct with three towers, with the Glittering Fen on one side and the Pileated Whiptail broodspire on the other. It's all boys of a certain age talk about, stealing a Whiptail egg and selling it to some Mrineen 'streamer and getting rich—

SA: I'm so sorry to interrupt, but you said "boys of a certain age." How old are you?

ZS: It doesn't matter.

Kiriki: She'll be eighteen in a month.

Zaya closes her eyes, squeezes her temples between fingers and thumbs for a moment, then opens them again.

ZS: Heart of mine, this is the second time you've taken a decision out of someone's hands because you didn't like their answer. Do we need to stop the interview and have a conversation, or can I count on your respect going forward?

Kiriki smiles sleepily at me.

Kiriki: She's going to be such a good mother. She *is* such a good mother. You can see it already. I carried this baby, but she's already teaching me lessons.

I hate to interrupt my subject in writing almost as much as I hate to do it in the moment, but it feels important to note that there was no discernible sarcasm here. Mrineen of my acquaintance would have used the same words to cut or parry; Kiriki, here, as far as I can tell, is sincere both in her meaning and her desire to communicate it to me, and by transition to you.

Kiriki: Yes, breath of mine. I'm sorry. You can count on me.

ZS: All right.

About three years ago, the Whiptail brooding season began, and we moved to the tenement in Cyan that was linked to our dole-flat. We landed in a four-family building with someone out of Chartreuse. That was around when the datura trade was getting started in Chartreuse, and our new housemate thought he'd drum up some customers close to home. Papa Kaalo got deep into it pretty quickly, and now we needed money and he was too twisted on datura to help Papa Zinji get it. So Papa Zinji brings me to the bay—they've been teaching me the basics for a couple of years now, but always with both of them connecting to the wyrm, they just let me... listen in. We've been walking half the day, not much to eat or drink because we're broke, we hit the beach just as the sun's going down, and the sand is packed and cool and just the best thing on my feet, and the last thing I can even think about doing is trying to wrestle my way into the brains of a killer lizard ten times my size...

... but I look up in the air and all that melts away, because there's this girl. Flying dragonback, skimming low over the water so I can see the shape of her, her hair flowing in the slipstream, taking this gorgeous Dawn Wyrm through the most graceful arcs I've ever seen...

At this point, your humble correspondent must disclose, Zaya has been progressively less and less able to suppress a burgeoning attack of the giggles; the last ellipsis above comes where she collapses into a full-on snort. Kiriki sighs.

Kiriki: She likes to do this because then I have to interrupt her and tell what really happened.

SA: I have brothers like that. I'm sorry.

Kiriki: I was, in fact, very much on the beach, not in the air. And on the beach, I was in the middle of receiving the Gift of Honeyed Verses from a boy I very much did not want to marry.

ZS, *giggling*: A Mrineen boy.

Kiriki: He was doing his best.

ZS: Kiriki kept the poem. It's like he never even read an actual Kayalim troth-verse… but he *had* read a few hundred novels written by Mrineen that had troth-verses in them, and none of those Mrineen novelists had read a troth-verse either.

Kiriki: What I'm going to do now is, I'm going to publicly shame my wife, in front of the entire circulation of your very successful newspaper. And she's going to let me do it, because she has no understanding of basic decency or generally of how to live in a society alongside other humans without being justly murdered for your crimes.

ZS: She agrees with everything I said about the poem. She just won't admit it in public because she's too nice.

Kiriki: While this poor, benighted boy was pouring his heart out to a woman he should have known better than to fall for, Zaya Shearwater comes over and says, "Do you actually want to suffer through the rest of this horseshit, or do you want to ride a dragon with me?"

ZS: And this little crowd-pleaser, who knows exactly what she wants and is desperately looking for a way to get it across without actually saying it, turns to her suitor, gives this shitty little shrug like it's out of her hands, and says, I quote, "An opportunity like that doesn't come along every day."

And this poor out-of-his-depth bastard turns completely blotchy, like he doesn't know whether to collapse or explode. And we'll never know what he *was* planning to do, because the Mule lands behind him and he takes off like a bottle rocket.

SA: And that was your first flight together?

Kiriki, *suddenly solemn*: No.

Zaya, too, becomes somber at this moment, her eyes hooded with guilt.

Kiriki: It's a fun story, up to this point. But you don't go up in the sky with someone who treats people like that.

ZS: She did come home with me that night.

Kiriki: But only—

ZS: —because she had nowhere else to go.

***

THE STORY OF HOW Zaya and Kiriki joined the 'stream is much less picturesque, by comparison: Kiriki didn't like the idea of thieving for a living, and her resistance gave Zaya the courage to say no and try another way. She began ground-crewing for other racers to earn pocket change and began to understand the world of the 'stream; she and Kiriki slowly strengthened their rapport with the Mule on later visits to the bay, and ultimately it consented to let them ride.

Kiriki will say almost nothing about her families, save that she has had many. She has never known her parents, and stayed with no foster family for more than two years; she emancipated herself earlier than was strictly legal, and refused to apply for a dole-flat. Her reasons were no clearer then, to her, than they are now, to me—if we are to believe her. She was content to confine her part of the story to after she met Zaya... though even there, as I review, Zaya did most of the talking.

***

ZS: MINSHOON WAS THE first to join us. He came to us with a fistful of sherds he'd won on some arbitrage on a couple of bets on the spread.

Kiriki: He said it was only fair—he'd studied a couple of our races and realized we were a little undervalued on courses with long straightaways and massively undervalued on races relying on maneuverability.

ZS: That was what kept us afloat while we were losing. And by the time the markets stopped discounting us for being a team and being Kayalim and being unknown, we had Cerminir and Kirono and Yyrreen, and we were winning.

SA: The markets have you favored to win the Bisai, with Arhoon Pogona and Harshaan Ora not far behind. What are their paths to victory?

ZS: What, you want us to tell our competition how to beat us?

SA: Why not? They'd be fools to believe you, wouldn't they?

ZS: ... you know what, fair enough.

Arhoon is flying an Argent Swordwing. His main advantage is the long straightaways, Tuatara Boulevard and the Esplanade of Stars and so on. He's been very careful to emphasize those in the qualifiers he's chosen... but this is a full-city race, and it'll be a lot of quick cornering in areas where buildings are low. Ice can build up a lot of speed with those huge wings and shoulders, but wingbeats that strong make it hard to go fast and still control your height. Swordwings are also good with cold, and I think Arhoon's counting on the Frozen Falls to slow us down more than him. Not a good bet, for my money.

Harshaan is flying a Dawn Wyrm about a cohort younger than the Mule, and raised to the 'stream. It's just a very solid all-around racer, and again, you can see that; Harshaan and Golden Hour have dominated every qualifier they've been in that we haven't. And we know Golden Hour's diet and growth are optimized in ways the Mule's aren't—because the Mule won't accept it, we can't afford it, and most of the work would have had to happen while it was second-cohort or younger.

Honestly, the way we've always beaten Golden Hour is on confidence. We'll take a turn closer to the corner, move faster down a narrow street, pass where it looks like it's too tight. Always take the little lead, let it add up.

Are you OK, heart of mine?

The change in Kiriki is unmistakable but subtle; I wouldn't have noticed it if Zaya hadn't called it out. Her arms are not smothering Jaliki, but they are tensed like iron bands around him, hard but gentle, her shoulders packed as dense as stone; her face is tautly blank, like a stretched sheet. If I look down, I feel certain I'll see her thighs and butt gathered in as if to leap up from her chair, her toes gripping the floor hard enough to leave track marks. She is braced to take a blow, or give one.

Kiriki, *smiling wearily*: Of course not. I pushed this one out of his house a month ago; I hurt from knees to nipples, and this poor homeless child wakes me up each night begging to be let back in.

ZS: Lesser women have suffered worse.

Kiriki: That may be, but their wives didn't force them to lead lives of crime on the backs of killer lizards feathered up like carnival clowns.

ZS: Neither did yours.

Kiriki: No, neither did mine. But that won't stop her from kicking me out of house and home if we lose. And I can't afford a second apartment.

Kiriki stands, careful not to wake Jaliki. She kisses Zaya, not long but not chastely either. Jaliki fusses; they separate; he settles. Kiriki turns to me.

Kiriki: You should write me as one of those sainted mothers. Glowing, beatific, serene. Write about how the bags under my eyes seemed to vanish when I was with my son, how the disarray of my hair seemed suddenly natural and perfect. Write me as a dessert, cream and coffee and chocolate, the way you Mrineen do.

SA: Why?

Kiriki: So this boy can read the piece you wrote, and the one they'll write about me after we win the Bisai. And laugh to think that two handsomely paid journalists could find such different ways to be completely wrong about his tired, saggy old mother.

SA: You don't think the article on the race will cover you as a dessert?

Kiriki: A comet-haired war goddess, I think. A radiant conqueror, her wyrm's colors flashing like flames in her eyes.

SA: I'll tell my editor.

Kiriki: See that you do.

***

I meet Arhoon Pogona on the patio of Tjaliraan's in Incarnadine Precinct; I couldn't afford to drink there, to the point where the bouncer would laugh me off the premises with a bullwhip, but they can afford not to serve gin in the morning, so the tables are unused and unpatrolled. It feels like this weird transgression is supposed to tell me something, but I'm not sure whether what I'm picking up is what Pogona's putting down.

Arhoon Pogona is not a member of House Shearwater, if the name of the city's third most powerful Great House left any uncertainty on that front. But it's a name I hear from every corner: 'streamers sublime and ridiculous, ground crews, bookies, fans, other journalists. He and Harshaan Ora, Zevjoon Anole, and Kanivoon Taipan have dominated the scene for years, since Kelloun Honu died and Jenirain Gila was crippled at the last Grand Bisai. No up-and-comer has posed a lasting challenge to the four of them, and their generosity in funding after-parties, prizes, and general operations has brought a mainstream appeal to the brimstone slipstream that 'streamers seem to regard, on average, as a kind of golden age. I am, as he approaches, ambivalent: I don't have a shred of standing to call bullshit on the 'stream's self-appraisal, but four well-off young Mrineen buying legitimacy for the scene they're lording it over doesn't sound like much of a golden age to me.

But what do I know? Everyone seems to be enjoying themselves, and whatever Pogona, Ora, Anole, and Taipan might have said or done—and they've said and done a few things—they don't seem to have impeded House Shearwater's trebuchet-like ascent to domination in the 'stream.

Back on the patio of Tjaliraan's, Arhoon Pogona pours himself into a seat across from me. He's handsome in a stringy, unshaven sort of way, with a wave of greasy hair that's greyer than it should be. He's got the leather jacket, the goggles are around his neck, and instead of a knife he carries around a longsword so massive the inevitable phallic jokes wilt in its shadow. When I stare at it, he waggles his eyebrows unsettlingly. He's not trying to harass me, I think, but I'm also not in the mood for this particular bit, so I go pleasantly for the jugular.

SA: Tell me about the Cold Point Chasse.

AP: I assume you mean "tell you about the first time Zaya and Kiriki spanked me."

SA: That's basically what I was after.

AP: They were the first 'streamers in history to bring back a live walrus-bat from Cold Point. It was a virtuoso performance. They deserved all the fame they got, then and later.

SA: At the time, you joined a complaint to the Standards Board about the use of psionics in the 'stream.

AP: Is that a question?

SA: Think of it as an invitation.

AP: All right. There was a race not long after, I forget which, and I was saddling Ice—

SA: —for our readers not following the 'stream, that's your wyrm, an Argent Swordwing—

AP: —that's right, and I was near the girls and the Mule, and it was the first time I'd gotten a good look at any of them. They're on top of the world now, of course, but back then, well... I don't mean to sound like the patrician twat I of course actually am, but their racing jackets weren't even proper leather, they were canvas, and their saddle-knives... I'm a decent judge of steel, and their saddle-knives could have taken kniving lessons from dole-kitchen silverware. They'll gut me when they read this, and I suppose they'll be right to, but it's the truth; to my own discredit, I just hadn't given any thought to how poor those girls were, and how much muck and mire they'd had to wade through to bring home that live bat at the Chasse. So I resolved that, if they lost the race, I'd buy them dinner. And they won, and I figured I'd do it anyway.

SA: You're widely respected in the 'stream, and in that scene you're viewed as a patron of House Shearwater—your opposition to various proposed empathy bans has been widely credited with the failure of those bans to gain traction with the Standards Board—

AP: That's kind, but they'd have failed anyway. Not popular enough.

SA: Not popular enough because you were against them, at least in part.

AP: I don't think people care that much what I think.

SA: That's an interesting point of view for a peer of House Pog-ona.

AP: Oh, those people care what I think. I meant real people.

SA: Real people care—you know what? It's fine. Look, before House Shearwater came on the scene, you were one of the top contenders to win the Bisai this year.

AP: Still am.

SA: But Kiriki and Zaya are favored against the field. My question is this: What do you say to the people who feel bringing House Shearwater in has made the 'stream less exciting, more predictable? Have you really just rejected the idea that psionic empathy is a special advantage that favors Kayalim 'streamers?

AP: I actually have. It's certainly no more powerful than money and spare time—and with a bit of effort, anyone can learn it; money isn't so obliging. It's no more powerful than me being able to ride Ice, which is an Argent Swordwing trained from birth to do high-speed maneuvers, instead of a scratched-up old barracuda-snatcher from the bay. And Kiriki herself has been teaching me the basics of empathy.

SA: Sounds like she doesn't have faith in your ability to beat her with it.

AP: No shit. But we all make mistakes.

Pogona says this last with an easy grin, and when I look at him like a livestock buyer eyeing a knock-kneed goat he splutters a little bit and says, "No, I didn't mean it like that!" He explains that it was just a joking way of saying that Kiriki Shearwater cares more about helping a friend than about securing her advantage in a race. I'm sure that's all it was.

***

IT'S A DANGEROUS HABIT to oblige one's subjects; you risk becoming their champion, or at least their mouthpiece, and it's difficult to shake that expectation from a source once it's taken root. But this much I think I can do.

The first reporting I did on the dragon-fliers of House Shearwater, before I talked to them at all, was the Mariposa Annulus, a long race through the peripheral precincts of Yemareir that begins in Violet Precinct and goes through the Rosewing Fountain in Cadmium. I'd been advised that this obstacle would be more challenging than the untutored might surmise—tight quarters, intermittent jets of superheated water, and butterfly-saturated air make for dangerous flying, and the butterflies' diet of sparklily pollen makes them prone to explode into corrosive clouds of ash when they catch fire. Rather than cover the starting line in Violet, which would have given me the chance to speak to the ground crew and Minshoon at the cost of a terrible view, I found a spot on a likely-looking ledge near the central geysers at Rosewing and settled in.

The Fountain is well attended at twilight in the early summer, and it's the crowd that first tells me the racers are approaching, first with murmurs and then with shouts. The approach to the Rosewing Fountain is Luthier's Row, wide and curved gently enough to let a wildebeest-chaser like a Ranger Wyrm build up a powerful momentum; and Tavisheen Slider's Ranger is named Searing Pursuit precisely for its feats of wildebeest-chasing, so it is a surprise but not a shock to see it wing into the Fountain perhaps a length and a half ahead of the Mule. The glint of tail-spikes on Searing tells perhaps a fraction more of the story; they are dangerous on any wyrm, but a creature of Searing's size and power could easily kill the Mule, which is two-thirds its size, with even a desultory blow to its head, neck, or shoulders.

I swear innovatively at myself—I've chosen this area because of its picturesque nature, but it isn't the sort of intricate map where the Mule and the doubled mind of its riders have an advantage. I'm only able to get through perhaps an oath and a half, though, before Searing banks hard, about to thread the needle between the Fountain's twin main jets, and a jet of fire leaps out to strike the edge of the mass of butterflies drifting lazily into the dragon's path.

This isn't an unknown tactic for 'streamers trailing in the Annulus; filling the air around your opponent with corrosive embers is not a bad way to slow them down. It's also an excellent way to injure or blind your own dragon. The slipstream of the lead wyrm will concentrate the burning particles in its wake, and the trailing wyrm, if it's close enough to execute this maneuver at all, is about guaranteed to sail face-first into the conflagration. It is, in short, a way to make someone else lose, but not a way to make yourself win. Which is why front-runners don't use it, which in turn is why front-runners don't fear it, or guard against it.

So Tavisheen Slider and Searing Pursuit are entirely unprepared to handle this loser's gambit; and, to their credit, they react rather well. Racer's leathers protect Slider's skin for the most part, although I will learn later that her hands are permanently pock-scarred from the butterfly-shrapnel that is, even now, immolating with a blinding jade flame. She protects her face by burying it in her arm; Searing, with no such options, merely closes its eyes, then howls with rage and pain as the ashes hit its wings and feathers. For a moment I see it covered with what seem to be a thousand emerald-rimmed holes. Then it skirls off to the side, crashing into a jet of boiling water thicker than its body. The force flings it perhaps half a length upward—above the disqualifying height, toppling upside-down, dumping Tavisheen Slider into a sakura tree—and as the Mule sails past, I take in all I can. The touch of its feathers seems to quench the jade butterfly-ash; its eyes are screwed shut, much as Searing Pursuit's were, although it flies blind with total confidence, trajectory and speed unaltered; and, though Zaya hunkers in the usual 'streamer's crouch at the base of the Mule's neck, where magenta feathers darken to violet, Kiriki is upright, craning her neck to see ahead. Her hair, jade green today, streams behind her like a comet; her arms are raised in exultation, and in exultation her mouth screams a scream that the slipstream takes for its own; her goggles flash in the dying cloud of bug-fire like the eyes of an war goddess.

***

ZS: WE DID THAT one to send a message.

Zaya waits a moment. I can't tell whether she's composing her thoughts or regretting having said as much as she has.

ZS: Tail-spikes and blades have been against regulations for over a century. That changed about three months ago—it wasn't even us, we were in the Bisai by then, but another Kayalim team on a cheap Dawn Wyrm used some tight finesse moves to edge out three top 'streamers in the Crevasse, and that was enough to get a foul cry from every weekend amateur who'd spent too much beer money on a juiced-up muscle wyrm. The Standards Board ruled that tail spikes and blades were legitimate countermeasures against overtaking, that anyone who was worried was free to buy armor, and that none of this was unfair because both spikes and armor would create drag and so it was all a tradeoff that would just introduce another dimension to the game—

—you probably know all this, right?

SA: I'd rather print your take than mine.

ZS: Your loss. Well, anyone who's watched more than five seconds of the 'stream can see where this is going. Precision overtaking is a major tool for lighter wyrms to gain an advantage; it's something cash-poor streamers can do, that Kayalim empath teams can do really well, and it's the only thing that makes the 'stream interesting at all past the ten-second mark. The Bisai is small this year, and part of the reason for it is the same set of Mrineen fuckboys—

Zaya sighs.

ZS: I'm letting my wife's taste for candor screw up my better judgment.

SA: I won't pretend I don't appreciate it.

ZS: Well, you see the problem. In the last three qualifiers, the top five 'streamers were the same—even though times went up by almost half a minute—because if you can prevent wyrms from passing you, all you really have to do is be first out of the gate.

The Mariposa Annulus was our answer to that. Tactics and precision maneuvers aren't afraid of your fucking tail spikes.

SA: Do you think the message has gotten across?

ZS: Honestly, I don't. Kiriki said that people would take it as a threat—if you do something House Shearwater doesn't like, House Shearwater will find a way to hurt you.

SA: That wasn't the message you intended?

ZS: No. The message was, if you prevent overtaking by threatening to maim and kill your competitors, we're *all* going to find ways around it, and some of them you might not like.

But to make it work, we had to do it with House Shearwater tools. Kirono used a fireproof wax, Cerminir fed the Mule up with a breath weapon diet to increase its range. So people see the threat as us, not the field. Just like Kiriki said they would.

SA: And you and Kiriki used psionics to fly the Mule blind?

ZS: We thought putting goggles on it might have tipped our hand.

A beat of silence, then another. Zaya is mulling over the wisdom of saying something. I bite my tongue.

ZS: Kiriki hasn't slept since that night. She says she dreams about the crash.

SA: I don't know what to say.

ZS: Here's what you should say. We're fighting for our lives here, every one of us who lives in this house. We are coaxing a giant killer lizardbird at lethal speeds through the air because that is somehow the most reliable way for any of us to get this *[she gestures expansively around herself]*, which something like half the Mrineen in this city have at any given time and three-quarters will at some point in their lives. And for the audacity of being better at it than they are, half of our competitors and the Standards Board feel, not just entitled, but *obliged,* to change the rules of the game we dominated to make it impossible for us and teams like ours to win unless we risk brutal maiming and death. We'll be the first in our families—since any of our ancestors came over from Kayazē—to cast a ballot for an alderwight because we're the first in our families to own property. We only own because we could race and win. So where the rest of this city sees a minor rule change in a game that's illegal anyway, we see a bunch of Mrineen putting their heads together to change the game that got us the vote, because they don't think we should be allowed to win it.

And yet, somehow, for not quite killing the opponents who'd have killed us without losing a wink of sleep over it, we stay up nights staring at the ceiling because it *is*, in actual fact, wrong to turn a cloud of butterflies into green fireworks when a human being's face is in the middle of it.

Even if I'd do it again without blinking.

***

I CAN'T GET ZAYA or Kiriki to escort me to Ashen Precinct before press time; but Arhoon Pogona will do it.

The border between Jet and Ashen isn't hard to spot, but you might cross it by accident if you weren't paying attention. The buildings in Ashen are lower, squatter, more weatherworn, more richly admixed with ancient structures—from the Vespertine Street approach you can see the massive lintel of a long-house. Which implies that the residents of the season-city did, at some point, try to live in Ashen Precinct; which perhaps constrains the timing of their migrations, since they wouldn't have built the Vore-wall if they had not had cause to run into a hatchling Vore. There's surely research on these matters, and someone will tell you about it... but not me: I'm writing these words with my ankle shackled to the largest desk at the Damask Free Press, a pen lashed to my hand and my eyelids pinned back like butterfly wings until I file. (My editor insists that I clarify that this is a joke, which I'll be happy to do as soon as he can spray a little water on my eyes so I can see the letters clearly.)

We get as far as the Vore-wall on Vespertine Street and I look into Ashen Precinct. I've passed by it more than once, but like most of the rest of you I avoid it even when the Vore brooding and hatching cycle has ended. I've never been inside. I look at the raised cobblestones that form the wall, separated from one another by about four feet. They rise about two inches from the street, which has clearly been rebuilt around them, with incised glyphs built up mostly of intersecting circles and squares, no two alike. Some bear flecks of long-worn-off ochre paint. There are three ranks of them, I notice for the first time, the two inner ranks several strides up the street and separated from one another only by a foot or two.

"Want to go in?" Pogona asks.

"Does it feel different?"

Pogona shrugs. "I'm the wrong person to ask. I lost a friend to Ashen Precinct."

This I have already learned from research. Kelloun Honu was the 'streamer favored to win the last Bisai; he was a few years older than Arhoon Pogona, but they had both come up through the Yemareir Air Guard. Both had flown Argent Swordwings rejected from service in the Guard because of minor physical infelicities; but while Pogona was struggling for traction in the 'stream, Honu had risen to rule it. Unlike Yymroun Tuatara, his body was never found, because no one today (bar 'streamers) is dumb enough to enter Ashen Precinct when Vore hatchlings are on the move. Since the Bisai is in a couple of weeks, it occurs to me that this would be an excellent way for Arhoon Pogona to murder me. Normally I'd crack a joke, but he's just referenced a tragedy.

"I'll go, but I'm sticking to the rings," I say.

He nods, and takes the step, and I follow, and then we take a few steps and cross the inner rings, and it feels like nothing. Still, I look back. Yemareir outside Ashen Precinct is higher, brighter, cleaner. Despite being just half a block away from Jet Precinct, despite seeing people and wyrms and monkeys in the street there, it feels deeply quiet, like being under a thick blanket in the middle of the night. I look up for any sign of wings or talons above us; nothing. We should have done that before we entered Ashen. We should leave. It's not safe.

"I should ask you something about Kelloun Honu," I say, "but what I really want to know is why Kiriki won't tell her story."

"She's tired. Jaliki was a difficult birth. She hasn't been sleeping well."

"Jaliki was a difficult birth? How so?"

Pogona shrugs. "Came out face up, I think? Or feet first. One of those."

"I've interviewed mothers of two-week-old triplets who were livelier."

"I'm not quite sure what you're after here."

I don't quite flinch, but it's an effort, because Arhoon Pogona's voice has gone as hard and sharp as a flake of flint.

I'm still sorting out whether to push or back off when he continues. "Sorry. It's just—your mothers of triplets haven't spent entire years fighting through everything this city and their own minds have thrown at them to get on dragonback week after week, and just lose and lose, over and over again, until they finally start winning. They haven't gone to these after-parties full of amateurs who are happy to pay to lose, week after week, when to you winning is the difference between... eating and not eating. Much less paying too much for bad beer and pretending to have fun. When winning is the one thing that can lift you out of this hole you're in."

"Are you happy?" I ask. "To pay to lose?"

He gives me one of those looks I can't help but be pleased with myself for getting, the one where you realize there's a fire ahead of you and a lion behind. "I'm a fortunate person," he says. "I can afford to lose."

"That's a long way of saying no."

"You're trying to make me say I don't want my friend to get what she's earned."

"Do you?"

Reader, he could just have said yes.

Instead, he rubs the back of his neck and looks away from me while he puts together what he's going to say. "I'm not happy to pay to lose," he says at last. "But one of us has to. Or both. It doesn't have anything to do with our friendship."

We both look down the quiet street into the heart of Ashen Precinct. The fastest route in the Bisai is this way: Vespertine Street to the broodspire, then out via Glaziers' Row. There's a scar on the cobblestones, a greasy black ash-stain the size of a horse.

"You're right," Pogona says after a bit, "she doesn't like to talk about her past. I know she was on and off work crews for a while, before she met Zaya. Took Cerminir to set her straight, if you can believe it."

I face a choice here. I want to ask Arhoon Pogona why Kiriki Shearwater, whom I know only as a tired, tiny mother suckling a skinny baby at a kitchen table, could possibly have been sentenced to hard labor *more than once*. And I am keenly aware that what I should do is not rely on hearsay: I should go back and ask her myself. And I am just as keenly aware that she certainly won't tell me.

I take the high road, and it leads where I knew it would. She couldn't meet before I had to file. I've got nothing for you, reader, not even hearsay.

Back in Ashen Precinct, feeling the cool, flowing pride of conformity to journalistic ethics, I spot a thing lurching through the sky like a goose taking off from a pond. It looks like a boulder, if boulders had legs and wings. Then it opens up what turns out to be a long, snaggletoothed jaw and flame flows from it. I expect a plume of dirty red but it's blue-white, pure and blinding, clean-edged like a dagger. I turn to Arhoon Pogona and half-expect to see him reach over his shoulder and rip the sword from its baldric, face down this fire-mawed killer like a fairy-tale knight.

He looks back at me with the same arch look he's had since I met him at the gin bar. "We're on the menu," he says. "Best make scarce."

We do.

***

THERE IS VERY LITTLE I can say about the ethics of covering a story like this that isn't already obvious to a reader of even moderate intelligence, except perhaps for this: It is a better thing to tell the story of House Shearwater, however flawed and partial the telling, than to let it go untold.

And that, in this grim twilight before my filing deadline, is the choice we face. I myself am out of time to cover the relationship between Cerminir's home, Cildinior Amalgam, and the city of Yemareir or the practice of the brimstone slipstream; and I am out of time to cover the middle seven centuries of the 'stream's history, which is of course the overwhelming bulk of it; still less do I have the time to hand these crabbed pages to an eager and crafty young Kayalim writer who could capture the nuances of House Shearwater's story that have escaped me. But let me offer this final observation.

Cerminir Shearwater left unanswered an elemental strategic question. Why feed a racing wyrm to spark change in its body, if the change won't bring more speed?

And here is the answer, in Cerminir's own words: You need an aversive mental experience of some kind. Dragons don't care if they lose a race.

Dragons don't care. But the Mule does. Because the Mule shares the minds of its riders, and its riders need to win to eat.

And I, at least, can't stop thinking: Is that the skeleton key to the success of House Shearwater, that their wyrm reshapes itself according to its riders' desires? Is it possible that Yyrreen, Kirono, and even Cerminir herself are nothing more than veils to obscure the outlines of the bone-deep biological advantage to which Zaya and Kiriki Shearwater have helped themselves?

Only time will tell—but not before the Grand Bisai. Yet the prospect has cast an off-angle light on all my thinking. At the outset of this essay—if, after all this, it still deserves the name—I gave Kiriki Shearwater a hard time for leaving her life as a glamorous dragon-riding criminal for the life of a house-poor domestic. That seems naïve and shitty to me now. But beyond my own blinkers and preconceptions, it feels like there's still another dimension to this purchase of a home, which brings Zaya and Kiriki to the polls for the first time.

Dragons are not the only creature requiring punishment to change. Government operates in the same fashion. And the government of Yemareir, like the Mule, is about to open its mind to Zaya and Kiriki Shearwater.

Analogies are fickle friends; but I suspect a fire-belching, feather-burning hellride is the very least we can expect now that these comet-haired war goddesses have got, or will soon have, the franchise. May it burn the wicked rather than the good, and arrive sooner rather than later; and may Minshoon Shearwater lose enough money on the spread that he never dares call Zaya and Kiriki Shearwater "overvalued" again, lest his creditors run his name through the muck of public opinion like the smug dog he is.

Yea verily, Minshoon, I think we will all learn something when we read this. Good luck to your family. They deserve it.

***

EDITOR'S NOTE: ON THIS seven-year anniversary reprinting of Shenireen Agama's "Face-First Into the Conflagration," we commemorate the deaths, shortly after this story saw print, of Kiriki Shearwater and the Mule, both killed by Cinereal Vore Wyrms in Ashen Precinct during the last Grand Bisai. They are survived by Kiriki's wife Zaya and son Jaliki, and her family Minshoon, Cerminir, Yyrreen, and Kirono, as well as children they preferred that we not name. We wish Zaya Shearwater the best of luck in her qualifying bid for this year's Grand Bisai.

***

SHENIREEN AGAMA IS THE Damask Free Press' senior reporter covering economics and culture. Her book on the history of Kayalim indenture and Kayalim ritual magic, *The Tusk-Mad*, will be available this summer. Her book on the brimstone slipstream, *The Linear Orchards*, has just returned to print.

Before you go

A QUICK WORD FROM your humble author. If you enjoyed this novella, I've got good news for you: The sequel, a full-length novel by the name of *Windburn Whiplash,* is available on all major retailers!
https://books2read.com/windburn-whiplash

And if you're reading this in November of 2024, **Windburn Whiplash is discounted to $0.99 for this month only!**

Interested in more of my work? Download my short fiction collection, *Remembered Air*, with a signup here:
https://www.cobblerandbard.com/mailing-list/

I email that list about monthly, with off-schedule announcements as I publish new work. I won't share your email with anyone.

Whether you sign up or not, thank you for reading! And, since this wouldn't be much of a series starter without an enclosed chapter of the next book... please turn the page for an enclosed chapter of the next book (that's *Windburn Whiplash,* available at the first link above).

Matt

WINDBURN WHIPLASH: CHAPTER 1

DRAGON. *ALSO "WYRM"; AFFECTIONATELY, "cargo parrot," "death chicken." In Yemareir and the surrounding area, a hollow-boned, winged, feathered, flying, fire-breathing reptile. Sociable and intelligent; innumerable species breed and live within the city limits. Named by analogy to a species of featherless reptiles (also with the fire breath, long extinct) used by the Empire of Mlinivoun to assert dominance over their territories, back when they had territories. The historical record indicates that the Mrineen who settled Yemareir had dreams of using the native wyrm population to resume their colonial bullshit, but—*

(We invite the reader to interpolate six eruditely referenced paragraphs of fulminating deletia on Mrineen colonialism. Please see Dr. Agama's widely praised articles, "Ectothermic Bastards of the Dragon Princes" and "Face-First Into the Conflagration," for more detail. —Ed.)

The main things for you, tourist, are these:

1. *Stay out of the precincts where breeding season is occurring. If you're in an area that doesn't look blighted, but the streets are empty, get out. If, in getting out, you run into a giant tower of obsidian and basalt that looks like the world's most evil termite mound, TURN AROUND.*

2. *Unless you want a pushy best friend with big teeth and no boundaries, do not feed these things.*

I'm not guaranteeing you won't get roasted and eaten if you follow these guidelines, but the probability will be much closer to whatever it is wherever you're from.

SEE ALSO: Brimstone Slipstream; Broodspire; Dragons, Common; Dragons, Rare.

—From "A Visitor's Handbook for Yemareir," by Shenireen Agama

***

There were a few ways to get hotter on dragonback than Zaya was in her third hour coasting over the Emerald Dunes—a direct hit from a geyser in the Mariposa Annulus, for one, or fifteen seconds coursing through the Devil's Tureen at an hour past noon. But when you were racing, there were other things on your mind, whether it was fending off the wyrm behind you or overtaking the one in front, and the rush of parting air keening a high white song the whole time. Out here, well—in theory, she was deeply absorbed in guarding the safety of the camel caravan below, stuffed with durable goods from Nistrium and the northern Ililuë convivencies. In theory, she was scanning for threats from all sides and triple-checking any shifty-looking clouds. In practice, all this vigilance occupied some small sliver of brain tissue deep in the back of her skull, leaving the rest of it free to dwell on every muscle moaning with the ache of spending hours clinging to a fire-breathing feathered lizard the size of an elephant.

She looked ahead at Vrinzhoon and Zrileen, sitting upright on blue-and-grey Dusk Stalker wyrms, and thought idly about whether she could shake them in a chase, and how long it would take. A wide-open course like this didn't reward agility; it would be purely an efficiency play. It wouldn't be hard to get them to waste their wyrms' blood sugar on extravagant sprints, pile up lactic acid in the muscles of their shoulders to slow them down. She could take this Dawn Wyrm anywhere and never get caught.

Or, anywhere except where the caravan was going to begin with: Back to Yemareir, to the house in Lilac Precinct, and to the purse of cash her family was waiting on. If they could afford to lose that, she wouldn't be here in the first place.

At the edge of Zaya's mind, she noticed the Dawn Wyrm notice a flutter of some kind in the corner of its eye, far above them.

"Don't chase buzzards," she said. "They're not good eating."

Too fast, the wyrm's mind responded. *Too big, too close.*

"How many?" Zaya asked. "What kind? Don't look up."

The wyrm waited several seconds, watching from the corner of its eye and tallying. *Maybe three.* The smell-image of the stalkers was thin, sharp, cold, the feather-pattern image grey-brown, the sense of size and mass substantial. Zaya put an image of a Greater Gyrdrake into the Dawn Wyrm's mind and got back a buzz of confirmation. *Your sense of smell is terrible.*

"Learn to add single-digit numbers and you can drag me," said Zaya.

The trajectories sharpened in her mind as they did in the Dawn's: Wide circular arcs, but moving forward, like a child drawing loops in a line, to keep up with the caravan, high enough that the clouds provided cover. Zaya slipped her goggles on and reached into her jacket to loosen the knife in the sheath against her ribs. "We're about to get hit." She imaged what she meant: Dragons plummeting from the clouds to crash into them with fire and talons, rag-clad bandits laying about with rusted bolos and machetes. "How would you get above a Greater Gyrdrake?"

Wait for it to kill another wyrm and land to eat it.

"Not an option."

Run away from it, go higher when it's out of sight.

"You're a shit tactician."

I don't eat Greater Gyrdrakes. I think maybe your friend there does though?

Vrinzhoon had his saber out and was pointing up at the sky; he shouted something to Zrileen, too far away for Zaya to hear. They peeled off and began to surge upward, broad wings and huge shoulders hauling them upward faster than anything that large had a right to move. The late morning sun caught them in stark shadows; they were beautiful sights, Zaya had to admit, tall, pale warriors with flashing blades, climbing upward through the sky on lithe, bright-feathered wyrms—their dorsal feathers straw-colored like the veldt, their bellies the color of the sky.

They're going to die, the Dawn Wyrm remarked in awe.

"Here's what we're going to do," said Zaya, and made an image of it for the dragon.

That's stupid, it said. *That's the kind of thing that gets you eaten.*

The gyrdrakes had stopped looping and begun to lose a little height, pulling slightly closer to Vrinzhoon and Zrileen. "Regret to inform that we are getting eaten one way or another if we lose this thing," said Zaya.

Not if we run away.

As one, the gyrdrakes fell into a stoop, gaping mouths belching cadmium-and-cerulean fire, plunging like knives down at the two climbing Dusk Stalkers—and at Zaya and the Dawn.

Its mind seized, frozen by the vision of the coming impact: flame stripping flesh from its face, talons and teeth parting feathers and flesh, blood bursting forth in rivers.

"It's OK," Zaya said, and *reached.*

In her mind, her own limbs doubled; she felt her own weight on her back, the push of massed air under her wings; her senses were overlaid with keen smell, dull hearing, a veil of slightly-off colors and contours in fine, swarming detail. She lashed her tail and hauled against the air, and the Dawn corkscrewed out and up, the gyrdrake missing them by inches.

The gyrdrake spread its wings to stop the fall, but Zaya had pulled the Dawn into its own stoop; and, before her wyrm could seize its muscles back from her control, it was on the gyrdrake's back, claws sinking into the grey feathers and then into skin, jaws locked around the joint where long neck met skull for control. Copper blood-savor filled the Dawn Wyrm's mouth, and Zaya's.

It wasn't enough to drown out Vrinzhoon and Zrileen's screams. She did not need to see the scene to know how it had gone; wyrm-fire had seared them to death, and the sheer force of the stoop had given the massive gyrdrakes every advantage, knocking the wind from the Dusk Stalkers and pitting them against a larger, more savage enemy face to face and from below. Whether they died valiantly or ran away would not matter much; in fact, a bandit of any sense would give them the opportunity to run, because—

—an odd sensation, referred from the Dawn Wyrm's belly: A tickling, almost, a scrabbling. The gyrdrake's rider, climbing from his own wyrm to hers.

Zaya's Dawn and the gyrdrake were plummeting toward the ground; the Dawn, at her urging, had pulled its own wings in, forcing the larger wyrm to do the work of slowing their descent. The Dawn's pink, blue, and violet feathers shone against the gyrdrake's dull grey; the bright red blood of the gyrdrake welled into a ruby bridge between granite-grey neck and magenta jaw; the gyrdrake's tongue lashed against the air as it bellowed its rage and terror. But the rider was coming, and they would be larger and stronger than her, and they would be better at clambering over dragons in midair than her, and better with a knife.

They hoisted themself onto the Dawn's back with a grace entirely out of place on this terrible plunge. They'd done this before. Zaya felt their body shift, felt the pain of their hand gripping her feathers—not hers, the Dawn's feathers—to steady themself while they drew a knife. She realized she had no idea what they looked like, save that their body was long-limbed and starved lean, and they were right-handed; she knew them only from the Dawn's referred sensations, not her eyes. They did not know she knew they were there. With a painful surge of will, she made herself not look as she felt them creep toward her.

"If this doesn't work," Zaya said quietly, "I'm going to need you to roast the gyrdrake's head."

If I do that, we're going to fall a lot faster.

"If you do that, you can let go of it and we can fly."

Why didn't we do that before this other human got up on my back?

"You're the one with its neck in your teeth! I can't do all the thinking around here!"

The gyrdrake's rider was in arm's reach of Zaya now. She *reached* for the Dawn, but didn't move it.

I don't like this. I don't like you in my head.

"You're alive because of me in your head."

The bandit's weight came forward on their feet, and Zaya lashed at them with the Dawn's tail.

It was not long or strong enough to knock them off—but the long orange feathers of the Dawn's tail-tip blinded them for a moment, and Zaya drew her knife and wheeled to stab them in the meat of their thigh.

It was an awkward stroke, without much strength in it, and it glanced off a strut of some hard substance sewn into the bandit's pants. She looked up into their eyes for a moment. The bandit was a Mrineen man, with the awkward tan of a human who's spent a long time outside in a climate his complexion hadn't evolved for. He was too thin, his teeth poor and partial, his hair weirdly well-kept. She felt his weight shift forward again, ready to swing, and thrust the Dawn's tail between his legs.

He buckled his knees in for protection, but she wasn't after the jewels. She switched the tail back as hard as she—the Dawn—could, swept him half off his feet.

She tucked her knife into her armpit, grabbed a handful of feathers with all the strength she could muster, and *reached* to release the flame from the Dawn's mouth.

The gyrdrake shrieked in agony and belched its own jet of fire, but its wings went slack before its voice gave out. The rush of air redoubled, and the half-pried-off bandit skirled off into the air.

"Letgoletgoletgoletgo," Zaya shouted, and after a moment's confusion the Dawn did, using its wings to catch the air and stop, at last, the roar of careering sky that would have spelled their deaths.

"Slayer of the Beasts that Haunt the Night," Zaya breathed, and before she could thank the god for their intercession, her sight went black with an impact that hit her like a brick house collapsing.

When her senses came back, she was falling, wedged between the Dawn's shoulder and its wing. Her arm burned with effort—not her own arm, but the Dawn's wing, which was pushing up in ways it wasn't built to do, keeping her just barely balanced on its back. The Dawn was snapping and shooting fire at a gyrdrake that had come at them from above, weaving back and forth to keep the bigger wyrm from gaining any more purchase. She felt the gyrdrake's talon graze her thigh.

She wrestled herself back up onto the Dawn's back, then felt something disengage from her jacket and fall away. She caught it by reflex; sharp steel bit her palm. She had not lost the knife.

The gyrdrake's talon was inches away from her. It could gut her with a twitch. Zaya grabbed its feathers anyway, pulled herself over the wing like a half-lamed sloth, felt the whistle of a blade lash past her shoulder blades, and severed the thong on the wyrm's saddle with a single stroke. She darted out of the Dawn's mind and into the gyrdrake's just in time to amplify the frequency range of the human voice: The bandit's plummeting shout echoed louder in the gyrdrake's brain than it had any right to do. The gyrdrake pushed off the Dawn like a hawk off a branch, following its rider.

Its talon snagged her jacket as it left. For a brief moment, it dragged her with it off the Dawn. Then she fell away.

Between her and the gleaming green sands there was nothing but air.

She knew she was falling, heard the slipstream roaring in her ears and tearing at her skin, but all she felt was a deep, suffusing stillness. There was nothing she could do.

What peace there was in that.

Her jacket jerked upward, the leather cutting into her armpits; weightlessness became weight, and her heart crashed against the cage of her ribs. The air stank of rotten eggs, and she heard the Dawn pant from above her: It had seized her jacket in its teeth. She laughed, high and hooting, tears steaming from her eyes. "Fseni-vain!" she said, *reaching* into the wyrm's mind as she said it.

What?

Zaya imaged Fsenivain and the Ranger Wyrm; she felt the Dawn twist its head to look up.

She's fine. The other wyrm is running away.

"You saved me."

The wyrm's mind acknowledged this, but seemed to feel no need to reply to it. Zaya looked down on the still-onrushing sands. Two bodies sprawled like dropped dolls; when she looked up to the horizon, she saw the dwindling forms of two gyrdrakes, headed west.

"They could have killed us."

Probably. But why?

"I feel like you're saying you wouldn't avenge my death."

I wouldn't avenge your death.

"My old dragon would have."

I can't keep flying with you in my mouth. I need to land.

"I know."

The caravan and the curves of the dunes grew as they descended, and the Dawn's hot breath stank, and the leather of Zaya's jacket cut into her armpits. She couldn't wipe the sweat from her brow for fear of slipping out of the jacket, so she let the drops form, swell, and fall, evaporating in the desert air before they hit the sand.

About the Author

Matt Weber is the author of the Streets of Flame series, *The Dandelion Knight*, *Reverie Syndrome,* and *Verso & Other Stories*, as well as short fiction in *Nature*, *Cosmos*, and *Kaleidotrope*. By day, he has worked in a number of data-related professions in academia, digital health, fintech, and government. He lives in New Jersey under a pile of writhing juvenile D&D addicts.

Bluesky: @mattweber.bsky.social
Mastodon: @mattweberphd@c.im
Instagram: @mattweberphd
Newsletter:
https://www.cobblerandbard.com/mailing-list/